P9-BZK-235

Sleepover Larry

by

Daniel Pinkwater

illustrated by

Jill Pinkwater

Marshall Cavendish Children

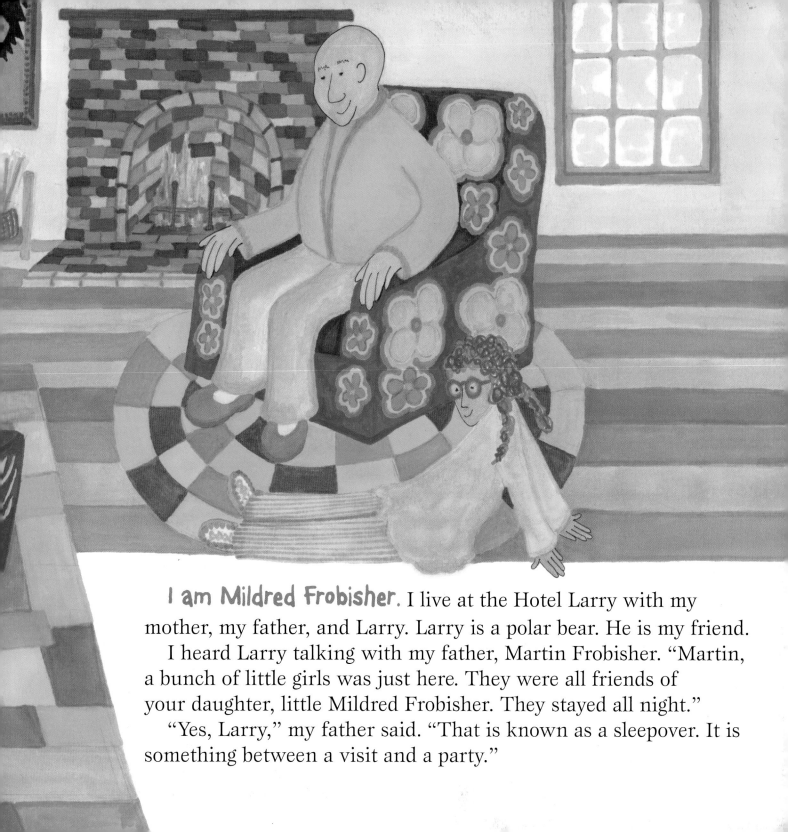

I am Mildred Frobisher. I live at the Hotel Larry with my
mother, my father, and Larry. Larry is a polar bear. He is my friend.
I heard Larry talking with my father, Martin Frobisher. "Martin,
a bunch of little girls was just here. They were all friends of
your daughter, little Mildred Frobisher. They stayed all night."
"Yes, Larry," my father said. "That is known as a sleepover. It is
something between a visit and a party."

"They stayed up late. They laughed and talked. They watched a scary movie. They had lots of snacks," said Larry.

"Yes. What prompts you to mention this?"

"May I have a sleepover, too? Could my brother, Roy, and the other polar bears come for a sleepover?"

"Larry, you are my best friend, and I named this hotel after you. Of course you may invite your friends to visit you."

Later, Larry came to my room.
"Little Mildred Frobisher, will you write
a letter and put a stamp on it and mail it?"
"Yes," I told Larry. "What will the letter say?"

"It is to Mr. Goldberg, the bear keeper at the zoo. Tell him I want my brother, Roy, and Bear Number One and Bear Number Three to come here and stay all night."

"I will write the letter and mail it," I said.

"Good," said Larry. "Then, will you help me prepare everything for the sleepover?"

"Yes."

"Good."

I asked Larry what food he wanted to serve at his sleepover.

"For supper we will have codfish cakes," Larry said. "And blueberries and muffins—blueberry muffins. For snacks we will have blueberries and codfish and maybe more muffins."

"Anything else?" I asked him.

"Yes. We will order pizza. Blueberry and codfish pizza with anchovies. Also, we will have ice cream."

"What flavors?"

"Blueberry. And codfish."

"And to drink?"

"Blueberry juice."

"Will you show a scary movie?" I asked.
"Yes," Larry said. "We will go to the video
store and pick one out."

"Anything else?"

"Yes. Do you think your mother, Semolina Frobisher, will let us use her record player and her old records?"

"I am sure she will. Anything else?"

"Yes. Do you think we can sleep in a tent on the hotel back lawn?"

"I am sure you can. Anything else?"

"I would like to invite you to the sleepover. Will you come?"

"May I have a flavor of ice cream other than codfish?"

"Yes."

"Then, yes."

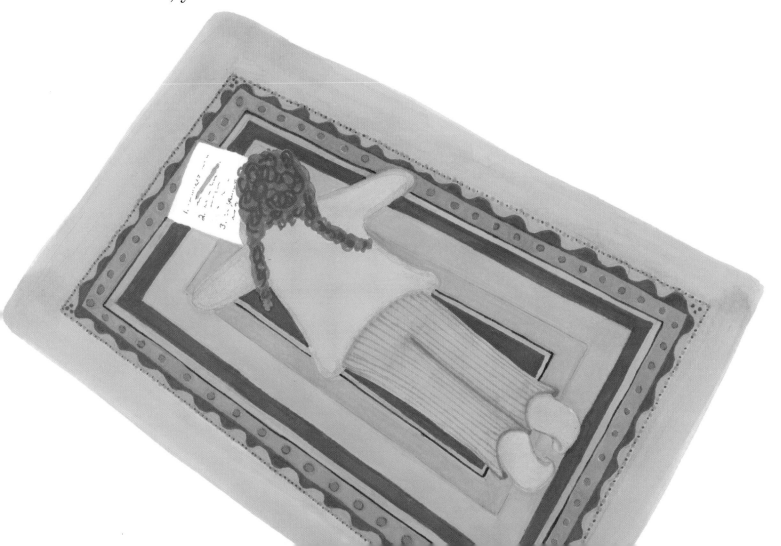

I went with Larry to the video store. He picked out a movie.

"I have chosen *Wild Polar Bears in the Frozen North*," he said. "It is a documentary."

"I thought you were going to show a scary movie at your sleepover," I said.

"This is scary," said Larry.

Mr. Goldberg, the bear keeper,
brought Larry's guests in the zoo bus.
"I am so excited!" Larry said to me.
"I have never had a sleepover before."

Out of the bus came Larry's brother, Roy, and the other zoo polar bears, Bear Number One and Bear Number Three. Each one had his pillow and his blanket with him. Also, a bunny and a wolf got out of the bus.

"We brought the bunny and the wolf," Roy told Larry. "They are friends of mine."

"I will come and get you all tomorrow," Mr. Goldberg said. "Be good animals, be polite, and have fun." Mr. Goldberg drove away in the zoo bus.

"Welcome to the Hotel Larry and to my sleepover," Larry said.

"We brought our pillows and blankets," Bear Number One and Bear Number Three said. "Should we go to sleep right away?"

"No, no," Larry said. "First, we are going to eat. Then, we will have all kinds of fun."

Bear Number One and Bear Number Three looked at each other.
"And we can stay up as long as we want," Larry said. "Also, there will be some surprises."
Bear Number One and Bear Number Three looked at each other again. "OK," they said.

I had supper with the animals. My mother makes the best codfish cakes and blueberry muffins. The bears had seconds, thirds, fourths, and fifths. The wolf wolfed its food. The bunny nibbled.

"While you are having your ice cream I will get the record player," Larry said. "Anyone who feels like dancing is welcome to dance."

Oh, the flat foot floogie with a floy, floy,
Flat foot floogie with a floy, floy,
Flat foot floogie with a floy, floy,
Floy doy, floy doy, floy doy.

He came a-walkin' and a-talkin', that grizzly bear.
He came a-huffin' and a-puffin', that grizzly bear.
Oh that grizzly, grizzly grizzly bear,
I said, that grizzly, grizzly grizzly bear.

The cat I love has got the blues,
'Cause his feet won't fit in his blue suede shoes.

He can wiggle his hips, wiggle his nose,
But the gals go crazy when he wiggles his toes.

The bears and the bunny and the wolf danced until they couldn't dance anymore. And I danced too.

When we were all danced out, Larry said, "More snacks!
And another surprise! We are going to see a movie!"
"Yaaay!" the animals said.
"It is a scary movie!"
"Yaaay!"

We gathered around the TV and watched *Wild Polar Bears in the Frozen North.*

"Is that Uncle Dave?" Roy asked. "That looks like Uncle Dave."

"Hey, look at that bear swimming!" Bear Number One and Bear Number Three said.

"Hey! Is that a walrus? Look what Uncle Dave is doing! Look, he's after the walrus! Run away, walrus! Run away! Oh no!"

"Eeeek! A bunny! No, Uncle Dave! Not the bunny! Oh no! Don't look! Eeeeek!"

I noticed that all the polar bears had their paws over their eyes. The wolf was sleeping. The bunny was munching blueberries.

"It was a scary movie," Roy said.

"We were not scared," Bear Number One and Bear Number Three said.

"The pizza is here! The pizza is here!" Larry said. We all had pizza.

"Ooh! Anchovies!" Bear Number One and Bear Number Three said.

"There is one more surprise!" Larry said. "We are all going to sleep in a tent on the back lawn!"

"In a tent?" Roy asked.

"Outside?" Bear Number One asked.

"In the dark?" Bear Number Three asked.

"Yes! It will be fun," Larry said.

"I am going to sleep in my room," I said.

I watched the animals go out to the back lawn. They were carrying their pillows and blankets and flashlights. I went to my room and went to bed. Before I fell asleep, I heard the animals outside. They were yelling and giggling and playing with the flashlights.

The next thing I heard was snoring. It was morning. There were four polar bears and a wolf sleeping on the floor of my room.

Larry opened one eye. "It got sort of . . . scary out there," Larry said. "So we came in here."

"Where is the bunny?" I asked. "I hope nothing happened to the bunny."

"The bunny is sleeping in the tent," Larry said.
"Nothing bothers the bunny."

We had breakfast. Blueberry pancakes with syrup. Then Mr.
Goldberg arrived in the zoo bus.

Larry and I stood on the porch of the Hotel Larry and waved
to the animals as they got into the zoo bus.

"Good-bye, Larry!" they said. "We had fun at your sleepover."

To Starr LaTronica, a great librarian, and Lulu, a great dog, both of whom encourage and help us —
in totally different ways
— J.P. and D.P.

Text copyright © 2007 by Daniel Pinkwater
Illustrations copyright © 2007 by Jill Pinkwater

Marshall Cavendish Corporation, 99 White Plains Road, Tarrytown, NY 10591
www.marshallcavendish.us/kids

Library of Congress Cataloging-in-Publication Data
Pinkwater, Daniel Manus, 1941-
Sleepover Larry / by Daniel Pinkwater ; illustrated by Jill Pinkwater.— 1st ed.
p. cm.
Summary: After little Mildred Frobisher has a sleepover at the hotel where she lives with her parents and Larry the polar bear, Larry decides
that he too would like to host a sleepover for his friends.
ISBN-13: 978-0-7614-5314-7
ISBN-10: 0-7614-5314-8
[1. Polar bears—Fiction. 2. Sleepovers—Fiction.] I. Pinkwater, Jill, ill. II. Title.
PZ7.P6335Sle 2006
[E]—dc22
2005020122

The text of this set book is set in 16 point Esprit Book.
The illustrations are rendered in pen and ink and colored markers.
Book design by Vera Soki
Editor: Margery Cuyler

Printed in Malaysia
First edition
1 3 5 6 4 2